FOR SALE

FOREWORD

EDWARD LEAR WROTE "THE OWL AND THE PUSSY-CAT" for a three-year-old girl named Janet. Her parents were friends of his, and he wrote in his diary, "Their little girl is unwell—& all is sad." To cheer her up, he created what he called a "picture poem."

That was in 1868. Some eighty-five years later, my grandmother read me the poem, and it still reminds me of her. Granny, after whom I was named Julia, lived upstairs from us and often read stories and poems to my sister and me. She had a collection of Edward Lear's poems and started us off on the limericks; our favorite one was about the old man with lots of birds' nests in his beard. We liked his rhyming alphabets too, and of course we loved all the made-up words. Who could resist runcible spoons and Bong-trees, and places like the Chankly Bore and the Jelly Bo Lee?

I think what I liked best about the longer poems was their spirit of adventure. So many of them are about characters who team up and set out on a quest: the Duck and the Kangaroo explore "the whole world three times round"; the Jumblies go to sea in a sieve; the Daddy Long-Legs and the Fly sail to the great Gromboolian plain to play battlecock and shuttledore.

Some of Lear's poems are tinged with sadness. The Pobble loses his toes when he goes to fish for his aunt Jobiska's cat, and the Dong with the Luminous Nose never meets with his lost Jumbly Girl. But "The Owl and the Pussy-cat" is an entirely happy story of courtship and marriage. Despite its humor and nonsense, the poem is charmingly romantic, from the Owl's

serenade on the guitar to the moonlight dancing in the last verse. I really like the fact that it is the Pussy-cat who proposes, and I am also fond of the other two characters in the poem, the Piggy-wig and the Turkey, who are both so obliging to the happy couple.

I had been married to my own Owl (well, he plays the guitar and acts as the owl when we perform *The Gruffalo*) for nearly forty years when I was invited to write a sequel to *The Owl and the Pussy-cat*. So I immersed myself afresh in Lear's poetical nonsense world and eventually came up with a story-poem that I like to think of as a kind of thank-you to Lear for giving me so much childhood pleasure.

Of course Lear illustrated his own verse. He was a serious artist, and even as he built his career as a nonsense writer, he always remained a painter, spending most of his life traveling, often to remote and wild places, to produce wonderfully fresh watercolor landscapes. For my sequel, *The Further Adventures of the Owl and the Pussy-cat*, I really wanted an illustrator who could capture something of Lear's sketchy fluid style without slavishly mimicking him. I was thrilled when Charlotte Voake, a watercolorist whom I had long admired, rose to the challenge. Charlotte, who turned out to be as great a Lear fan as I am, did a wonderful job creating not only the new characters but also the Owl and the Pussy-cat themselves.

I was delighted when I heard that Charlotte would also illustrate an edition of the original poem by Lear, and she has captured his humor and poignancy perfectly. Although "The Owl and the Pussy-cat" was recently voted Britain's favorite children's poem, I sometimes fear that it is more familiar to grown-ups than to children. I hope that this beautiful book will change that.

Julia Donaldson

For my family
C. V.

"The Owl and the Pussy-cat" was first published in
Nonsense Songs, Stories, Botany, and Alphabets (London: R. J. Bush, 1871).

Foreword copyright © 2014 by Julia Donaldson
Illustrations copyright © 2014 by Charlotte Voake

Published by arrangement with Puffin Books, part of the Penguin Group
First U.S. edition 2017

Library of Congress Catalog Card Number pending
ISBN 978-0-7636-9080-9

16 17 18 19 20 21 APS 10 9 8 7 6 5 4 3 2 1

Printed in Humen, Dongguan, China

This book was typeset in Berkeley Old Style.
The illustrations were done in pen and watercolor.

Candlewick Press
99 Dover Street
Somerville, Massachusetts 02144

visit us at www.candlewick.com

The Owl
and the
Pussy-cat

EDWARD
LEAR

illustrated by
CHARLOTTE
VOAKE

With a foreword by JULIA DONALDSON

CANDLEWICK PRESS

The Owl and the Pussy-cat went to sea
In a beautiful pea-green boat,

They took some honey, and plenty of money,
Wrapped up in a five-pound note.

The Owl looked up to the stars above,
And sang to a small guitar,
"O lovely Pussy! O Pussy, my love,
What a beautiful Pussy you are,
You are,
You are!
What a beautiful Pussy you are!"

$Pussy$ said to the Owl, "You elegant fowl!
    How charmingly sweet you sing!
O let us be married! Too long we have tarried:
    But what shall we do for a ring?"

They sailed away, for a year and a day,
To the land where the Bong-tree grows,

And there in a wood a Piggy-wig stood
With a ring at the end of his nose,
His nose,
His nose,
With a ring at the end of his nose.

"Dear Pig, are you willing to sell for one shilling
Your ring?" Said the Piggy, "I will."

So they took it away, and were married next day
By the Turkey who lives on the hill.

They dined on mince, and slices of quince,
Which they ate with a runcible spoon;

And hand in hand, on the edge of the sand,

They danced by the light of the moon,

The moon,

The moon . . .

They danced by the light of the moon.